FOR MY LOVING SONS
RYDER AND RAYCE

WHAT WOULD YOU DO....

BECAUSE YOU HAD RAZOR SHARP TEETH

WHAT WOULD YOU SAY
IF EVERYONE SWAM AWAY

JUST BECAUSE THEY SAW YOU BENEATH

BUT DID YOU EVER STOP TO WONDER

ABOUT THE FEELINGS HIDING UNDER THE SKIN OF THE SHARKS ON THE REEF

I BET IF YOU DOVE DOWN DEEP
TO WHERE THE SHARKS ALL SLEEP

YOU'D SEE
ANOTHER SIDE
TO THIS TALE

THERE'D BE NURSE SHARKS WORKING HARD.

BLACKTIPS AND MAKOS
PLAYING CARDS

AND EVEN
A HAMMERHEAD DRIVING NAILS

THERE'S A GREAT WHITE SHOWING OFF IT'S POWER
TO A LEMON SHARK WHO'S LOOKING SOUR

THEY'LL BE HAPPY AND GLAD
BUT SOMETIMES THEY GET SAD
AND HIDE THEIR TEARS IN THE DEEP BLUE

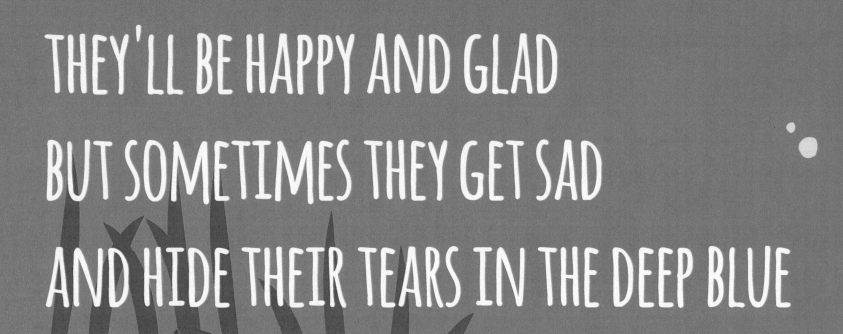

THEY HAVE A MOUTH FULL OF TEETH
AND FEAST UPON FISH AND MEAT

AND AREN'T THAT DIFFERENT THAN ME AND YOU

SO IF YOU SEE A SHARK SWIMMING ABOUT
DON'T SCREAM, CRY, OR SHOUT
THE BEST THING TO DO
IS KEEP DISTANCE BETWEEN YOU

AND REMEMBER THAT SHARKS HAVE FEELINGS TOO

CPSIA information can be obtained
at www.ICGtesting.com
Printed in the USA
LVRC091509220721
693422LV00002B/30